AMRRUT SARAVANAKUMARAN

The Space Adventures

The Destruction of the Pirates
Book 1

Editing by KarolynEditsBooks.com

Table of Contents

1 - What Just Happened at School?   1

2 - Science Class   7

3 - Lunch Time   11

4 - Lunch Recess Turns into an Adventure   15

5 - Dang It! Darn It! They're Here!   21

6 - Escape and News Time   27

7 - Follow the Clues   31

8 - The Battle of the Diamond World   37

9 - Thomas vs. Captain Renshaw Vance   43

10 - Tryphone vs. the Master Gunner   49

11 - Friends Reunite   53

12 - On Our Way Back Home   57

13 - Home Sweet Home!   61

About the Author   66

CHAPTER 1

What Just Happened at School?

It was just another uneventful morning on Mars. Yeah, good ol' Mars. I was fast asleep on my bed, but would soon be very embarrassed.

You see, yesterday my friend, Tryphone (pronounced try-phone) came over for a sleepover. We've been friends since I was five when we discovered that we were neighbors and went to the same school.

Honestly, it was my first sleepover with him so I wanted to impress him by showing him that I was a responsible and disciplined makid (a kid on Mars). I also wanted to show him that I am a makid who wakes up on time. Waking up on time is really hard, you know… gotta give yourself a pat on the back if you can do it. So, I decided to set an alarm for 5:00 a.m. I have to leave for school at nine, and school starts at ten. It's not my fault I take three hours in the bathroom.

Well, as you can guess, it wasn't pretty. The alarm startled me and I fell off my bed and landed on my Lego masterpieces and screamed, "No! My masterpieces! Yikes! Ow! That actually hurt! Help! Owie! Help me, Mama!" and started crying in front of Tryphone. So what if I cried so bad! I'm puny! It hurt, you know? I also felt so bad that I'd fallen on my masterpieces. I worked so hard on them! Making them took hours! Ow! My bottom hurt!

I shouldn't have cried—well, you know why. First, Tryphone was unimpressed with me, and second, my parents came running.

"Aww sweetie, are you okay? Are you okay, my poor little darling? What happened to you?" Mom said in that annoying voice.

That was too embarrassing. Tryphone started smirking at me. Turned out that I was also drooling... Worst and most embarrassing way to start the day.

By the time I felt better, it was already six o'clock! One whole *hour* had passed by! I rushed into the bathroom, brushed my teeth and took a bath. I'd been too lazy to get a towel, so when I was done, I screamed, "Mommy! Gimme a towel!" When my mom came to bring me the towel, I snatched it and dried myself. I put on my school uniform, then had to take it off and put it on again because it was inside out... too much work!

When I came out of the bathroom to eat breakfast, it was already nine o'clock! I ate breakfast as fast as I could, but it still took me almost an hour. My dad had already dropped Tryphone at school and was back and now waiting for me.

It was almost ten o'clock when I stepped into the car with my thirty-five-pound backpack. (Why was it thirty-five pounds? Maybe because my parents packed a safety kit, extra clothes in case I have an accident, extra water bottles, gloves to stay hygienic, extra socks, and you know what? That's enough. Wait, did I just tell you why it was thirty-five pounds? Oh, darn. Just don't tell anyone!) My dad drove one hundred miles an hour just to get me to school faster. I finally reached school at 10:30, though recess had just ended. Dang!

I got yelled at by the teacher for coming late. While she was yelling at me, my worst enemy, Benignus (a bully whose name literally means "kind" in Latin), whispered, "Boo!" in my ear.

This spooked me a lot and I screamed, "Ah!" and fell off my chair. I started crying...

Then one of the girls yelled to me, "Hey Thomas, why don't you get your backpack where you always have a safety kit? " (By the way, my name is Thomas, in case you didn't know.)

Well, everyone including the teacher laughed at me (thank you teacher, very much; laughing at me was very, very helpful) but Tryphone didn't.

I *did not* think that I would actually go run to my backpack for the safety kit, but I actually *did* make that puny choice. When I opened my backpack for the safety kit, all my extra stuff poured out and everyone except Tryphone laughed *again*! Obviously, I had to clean the mess up. Whatever! After cleaning it up, I sat back in my seat, where someone had put one of those whoopie cushions. I got laughed at yet *again*! I threw that cushion in the trash for good, and then went back to my seat.

It was math time (my favorite subject). The first question assigned by the teacher was, "Thomas arrived how many minutes late to school? How many minutes later did he sit on the whoopie cushion? How many minutes before that did he fall off his chair and start crying?" Well, I guess it was a math problem because it included the word "minute."

Next problem: "X to the power of N plus Y to the power of N equals Z to the power of N." Impossible to solve, right? Worse, the problem was only for me and if I got it wrong, I would have to go to the principal's office and tell him why I came late to school. I also had to do one thousand push-ups and sit-ups in one week! Crazy, right?!

Next it was writing time. The prompt for our essay: "Write an essay describing why Thomas came late to school. If you don't know, make up your own funny reason." What did I do for *my* essay? I made up my own reasons and blamed my parents. Fortunately, the teacher did not tell my parents about the essay.

The Destruction of the Pirates

CHAPTER 2

Science Class

The next day started off pretty well. The teacher came late, and we waited for her. When she entered the classroom, she was all wet like she'd just taken a bath, but with her clothes and glasses on. Apparently, it was raining heavily. If you're wondering how it rains on Mars, well, I learned about that in science class. My notes are on the next page.

I know it says "Mars History"—I was too busy thinking about what I got for lunch. Should it be "Mars History-Science," I guess? 'Cause it's the history of when Mars was terraformed and the history behind Mars, but it is also science class. School is very confusing and weird here on Mars! I bet it's way better back on Earth. I even heard that they've got these cool animals like the small black thing that flies... What's it called? Oh yeah, a kroe. No wait, sorry—crow. Oh, and alligators, sharks, whales, squirrels, and cats! They say that cats are kept as pets! They do look cute.

Thomas	**MARS HISTORY**	**8/30/13024**

Mars has been terraformed into an Earth-like paradise.

By reestablishing a magnetic field to protect Mars, thickening the

atmosphere, removing perchlorates from the soil, creating an ozone

layer, and adjusting the atmosphere, we have terraformed our red

planet into an habitable paradise. Our terraformed planet, Mars is

still very different from Earth. Our days and years are longer. the

gravity is lower and the climate is very different. Terraforming

Mars took thousands of years, and required technology, and

megaprojects. Scientists contemplated building greenhouse gas

producing factories that generated large quantities of methane

chlorofluorocarbons, and carbon dioxide, which would then trap solar

radiation and helped build a thicker Martian atmosphere.

The only pet that we can have is a limosatardus! It was created during Mars's terraformation, according to my science teacher. My science teacher says that in Latin, *limosa* means slimy and *tardus* means slow. It literally translates to slimy slow in Latin. How gross!

I learned in science class that there are things that are slimy and slow on Earth too, and some are also kept as pets. They are called earthworms. Okay, let me just summarize what I learned about earthworms. Earthworms are slow and slimy creatures around the size and color of a pinky that live under the ground. They fertilize the soil with their feces, aka excretion. This allows plants to grow healthier. If you cut a worm in half, some species regenerate a tail. For other species, the tail side regenerates a head, and the head side regenerates a tail. This creates two worms, but the tail side might also regenerate another tail, and then it wouldn't survive. Pretty cool, right? Mars doesn't have anything like that! NO FAIR! But we do have the limosatardus, which Earth *doesn't* have.

I also learned some cool facts about Mars. Did you know that Mars is smaller than Earth, with a diameter of 4,217 miles? This makes it the second smallest planet in our solar system! One day on Mars lasts about twenty-four hours and thirty-seven minutes. And one year on Mars is 687 days long! That is 1.9 times as long as an Earth year. This is because Mars is farther away from the Sun, so it takes longer to orbit it.

Okay, that's it, no more science stuff. I'm D-O-N-E! DONE! Well, since science class finished five minutes ago, LUNCH TIME!

CHAPTER 3

Lunch Time

Yay! I got my favorite food! Sexagintaquadruple-cheesy macaroni and cheese, with extra cheese. "Miss Lunch Teacher, may I please have five parmesan cheese packets?"

"Yes, you may."

"Fpanks da flot!" Sorry about that, my mouth was full. By the way, if you're wondering, *what in the world is sex-a-gint-a-quadruple?* You know how there's single, double, triple, and quadruple? Following that same logic, for sixty-four of something, you would say "sexagintaquadruple." That word hasn't been invented yet—wait, actually it has been, by me! You know, I am pretty smart...

"Food fight!" someone yelled out. Oh great, how will I enjoy my sexagintaquadruple cheesy macaroni and cheese with extra cheese and another extra five packets of parmesan cheese?! Whatevs... I guess I'll just hide under the table and enjoy my lunch. Oh no! Benignus is coming toward my table. Yeah Tryphone threw his hot sauce balloon at Benignus's face. Way to go, Tryphone!

By the way, Tryphone is *known* for his hot sauce balloon. His mom tries to make sure that he survives every food fight during lunch, so she packs him several gallons of hot sauce ammo every day. And did I mention? One hundred balloons. Each balloon can cover a person's whole face with hot sauce once it touches their face. Several gallons of hot sauce equals one hundred full balloons.

Tryphone and I were always on the same team in food fights. Everyone usually had a tray for a shield and some kind of face covering on whenever Tryphone is around. Luckily, this time, Benignus didn't see Tryphone, and didn't have all of his shielding stuff.

Benignus couldn't talk because of the spice in his mouth, couldn't breathe because of the hot sauce in his nose, and couldn't see because of the hot sauce under his eyelids. Well, that's what he gets for being such a bully! Plus, Tryphone won't get into trouble because it was a food fight, and Benignus started it.

And now, Benignus was getting taken to the school nurse and scolded for starting the food fight. The real good part is when the school nurse is like, "Aww sweetie, are you okay? Are you okay, my poor little darling? What happened to you?" in that annoying oice. That was too embarrassing for Benignus. But he was getting ll kinds of treatment and blah blah blah.

Aaand, the food fight continued.

Benignus's friends, Cosmo (his name means "order, rganization, and beauty" in Italian), and Deacon (his name means dusty one, servant, and messenger" in Greek) were our new nemies now. Such weird and lame names! Why would a parent ame their son beauty, dusty one, servant, and messenger?

Well, apparently, while everyone was watching Benignus go o the nurse's office, Cosmo and Deacon were busy switching their mmo with a bunch of Tryphone's hot sauce balloons. So when we vent back to the lunch room, we were left with two trays, two hot auce balloons, a whoopie cushion, two ropes, and fifty bottles of owdered parmesan cheese.

While everyone was busy food-fighting each other, Tryphone nd I were busy food-fighting Cosmo and Deacon. We were ctually pretty smart (actually I was), and I filled the whoopie ushion with parmesan cheese and squeezed it right in front of heir faces, so it puffed out like smoke and they couldn't see a hing, except parmesan dust or whatever.

Then I quickly pulled Tryphone under a table with me and ising the two trays, I made sure to block the area under the table vhere we were. Our two enemies couldn't see because of the smoke, so they threw all of the hot sauce balloons all around them until they had none left.

When the smoke cleared out, we cornered both of them against the wall in a way that kept them from running away. And here's the cool part: we quickly ran back as fast as we could, then we turned around and threw our two hot sauce balloons at their faces.

After that, we sprayed more powdered parmesan cheese at their faces so that their faces were completely white. For the final finishing touch, we poked two dots on each of their faces in the powder for two red eyes, and drew frowns and big, weird red noses. Best painting-on-a-human-thingy ever!

Then, we tied a rope around their arms so that they couldn't smudge the "art" on their faces and carried them to the school nurse's office. The school nurse asked, "Aww sweeties, are you okay? Are you okay, my poor little darlings? What happened to you two?" in that same annoying voice. That was too embarrassing for Cosmo and Deacon.

CHAPTER 4

Lunch Recess Turns into an Adventure

Lunch recess—yaaaay! Our longest recess. It's forty-five to sixty minutes long! And this lunch recess is going to be one of a kind—no bullies! A bully-free, one-hour-long lunch recess.

"Lava monster!" I screamed. I ran up the play structure and was about to slide down the slide when I stepped on something. I couldn't see what it was or where it was. But it felt like some sort of invisible, top-secret button. And then, there was a one-minute countdown that nobody but me seemed to be able to hear.

I quickly slid down and ran off to find Tryphone. In less than a minute, we were back up there. With five seconds left in the countdown, suddenly, two robot arms zoomed out of the play structure and put some type of eye lens on each of us. I could see the invisible button!

Then, something else came out of the play structure—no, the play structure transformed! Things just kept getting better and better! Apparently, we were wearing lenses that could see stuff that was normally invisible to the naked eye.

We went through a door that had appeared, and the door closed behind us. This place looked like an S.S.A.B.! I learned from our science teacher that an S.S.A.B. is a spaceship assembly building. Basically, it's where scientists build spaceships.

It looked so cool! The room we were in looked very adventurous. We saw a bunch of computers, racks containing subsystems and cool gadgets, work stations, stowage lockers, supplies, equipment, and experiments for all the missions. I got the urge to hop into the spaceship right beside me and just BLAST OFF!

Well, the next thing I knew, I was sitting in the pilot's seat inside the spaceship and Tryphone was sitting in the copilot's seat. My heart was pounding hard; I was nervous but also excited. The ceiling opened, and speakers counted down, "10...9...8...7...6...5...4...3...2...1...0... BLAST OFF!" I pressed the blast-off button, and we zoomed into the air!

As the spaceship rocketed up, we realized that we didn't have our spacesuits on! We tried to unbuckle our seat belts to put on the spacesuits, but the ship wouldn't permit us to unbuckle while we were still headed toward space! Luckily, we stayed safe and didn't get hurt.

Finally, we reached space! We unbuckled our seat belts and drifted towards the racks where the spacesuits were. We put our new spacesuits on, which wasn't easy. Then, we sat back in our seats because we were too scared to even think about going outside of the spaceship.

Then Tryphone started shivering, his teeth started chattering, and he turned pale. Even his eyes started watering. "What's the matter?! Why are you freaking out?" I asked him.

He replied, "Th-th-the s-s-space p-p-pirates! They m-might b-b-be here!"

You see, space pirates have always been a big problem. The solar system military (S.S.M.) is always struggling to deal with space pirates. Any spaceships traveling in outer space always need to be protected by at least five military spaceships because several space pirate gangs attack spaceships and steal from them. Space pirates have also fought many wars with the S.S.M. The S.S.M. usually receives assistance from Mars Space Patrol (M.S.P.). They also get help from the Solar System Patrol (S.S.P.), the Earth Space Patrol (E.S.P.), the Earth Military Defense (E.M.D.), and the Mars Military Operation (M.M.O.). Even with so many combined forces, the space pirates often win because many gangs team up during these wars. But sometimes, different gangs battle each other.

On top of that, several planets, private military operations, and space bases in the solar system have been attacked by space pirates.

The space pirates rarely failed. The few times they failed was only because some shady space operations (meaning those involved in both legal and not so legal operations) offered the pirates money to either retreat or let their target "win."

Now, Tryphone freaking out was one thing, but freaking me out too was a whole 'nother thing. We had to do something to protect ourselves. We had a plan. We would turn on all of the

cameras on the ship, and if we saw another spaceship getting close to us, we'd set our spaceship at full speed and try to escape. If we are unable to escape and they tried boarding our ship, we'd continue at full speed, then keep spinning until we shook them off.

If they were still somehow able to stay attached to our ship, we'd brush against *their* spaceship hard enough so that their own spaceship would knock them off. Then we'd escape as fast as we could. If they caught up to us, we'd immediately land back on Mars. But we'd only do that if they found us.

But meanwhile, we'll just relax, explore, and enjoy outer space... or should I say, Chillax...

CHAPTER 5

Dang It! Darn It! They're Here!

As we ventured through this phenomenal part of outer space, something seemed to be missing—we felt like we were doing something wrong. But then again, we're kids and we're not supposed to be out here in outer space. We were probably just not used to being up here.

We got the feeling that something or someone was following us, but again, in outer space, there is a lot of space junk and asteroids that might just be drifting behind us. I remembered something my science teacher said, something like, "Things just don't follow you." Yeah, whatever. Probably didn't matter now.

I *knew* something was wrong, there's something we weren't doing, something we weren't aware of. I felt like my subconscious was trying to tell me something, and now, it was just getting too annoying! *WHAT IS WRONG?!*

All of sudden, an incoming transmission blared through the speakers: "Now we shall jus' take down that ship 'n plunder all o thar goody goodies! Har har har! Or we might jus' use thar ship as our ship 'cause 'tis better than ours. We shall make those passengers in thar our cabin boys! Come on, ye space dog. 'Tis not enough rum in the world to make yer face look good, ye cheatin space dog! Press the hoist the anchor button! Board thar ship!"

"Dang it! Darn it! They're here!" I screamed as I tried to do something, like execute the plan. But they were already too close. I checked the cameras, and discovered they were all off. How did that happen? That's probably why I'd felt like something was wrong because the cameras had been off and they **WERE** following us. I turned the cameras back on.

"Pirates!" Tryphone panicked.

It was Plan B time, as if we had a Plan B. "Tryphone! Pirate time! Its time for *us* to be the pirates, not them! Board thor, no thar ship!" Next time, I'll just stick to normal English.

"Wait, what?" yelled Tryphone.

"Yes, we attack the attackers! Are you ready sir, for this important and significant mission? Some of us may not even return," I said. "We take them down from the inside!" I declared like a well-trained, professional soldier.

We exited through the emergency hatch on the side of our ship that the pirates couldn't see, so we could sneak around the back and onto the space pirate's ship (I was like an OP ninja, FYI).

Once we got inside their ship through an unsecured hatch, we overheard their conversation. "Wha' takes ye so long jus' t' board thar ship! Yo har har har an' a bottle o' rum!"

"Cap'n, thar seems t' be no space dog in that ship," the boatswain said to the captain.

"Master Gunner, destroy that ship! Then collect all the goody loot! All fer me! Har har har!" ordered the captain.

"Aye aye, Cap'n! I be on it! " said the master gunner.

"Quick! Hurry up! Do it fast, ye space dog! Arrr!" said the captain.

Oh no! We had to do something quick or else we end up getting caught and being punished by these pirates or we might be stranded in space.

"Psst, Thomas," Tryphone whispered.

"What?" I whispered back.

"Attack them so they don't destroy our ship," he whispered.

"No, they're stronger than us and we might lose our lives and our ship," I whispered back. "Quick, let's sneak back onto our ship and speed off before they catch us," I said.

"Boatswain, Master Gunner, shhh, be quiet," said the captain. I reckon someone be in our ship, spying. Be careful, 'ave yer pistols ready."

They knew we were there! Well, that might be a good thing because it would take longer for them to destroy our ship. We had a chance. "Quick, let's get out of here," I told Tryphone. As we hurried toward the door we'd snuck in, a pirate caught us.

I found a pistol laying on the floor, so I aimed it at him. He said nothing and put his hands up and dropped his weapon. Tryphone caught the pirate's weapon so it wouldn't make any noise. I kept the pistol aimed at him, then we quickly exited, and jumped back into our ship. We sped off at full speed, all the while hearing the pirate captain screaming at us and his crew through the speakers.

We could make out bits and pieces. "Ahoy, har har har, ye squiffy, floggin', ole salt! Listen bucko, ye chimp-faced, mutiny-startin' spacedog! ... Ahoy! Ye lost t' two wee sprogs?! Ye fight like a dairy farmer, ye wee' space dog! ... Strike yer colors! Ye fight like a rodent, ye wee', bloomin' space snake! 'Tis the Black Spot fer ye, ye rodent! ... Yo har har har an' a bottle o' rum. Ye fork-faced, pox-ridden, crud bucket ... Blimey!"

After that, I'd had enough, and didn't bother to try to listen to anymore of his insults.

The Destruction of the Pirates

CHAPTER 6

Escape and News Time

They were catching up, really fast! They were only a few hundred feet behind us, and we assumed the master gunner was ready to launch MISSILES! We had to do some-thing, and fast.

I looked at all of the buttons, confusing screens, and controls, and found something called "Light Speed." I pressed it and was asked for a location, so then I chose a dot on the map, probably just a random place in the solar system.

I think I made a mistake because only 3.75 seconds had passed on the spaceship's clock, but according to the ship's computer, 2.25 years had passed on Earth and *4.23 years* had passed on Mars! This was due to the percentage of light speed the ship had traveled at and effects of time dilation.

Oh well. Now it was time to just sit back, relax, and enjoy a TV show on one of the ship's screens. Time to watch the news.

"Recently, a band of space pirates have been boarding smaller ships traveling in this area of the solar system," said the news reporter. "They call themselves, 'The Legends of the Galaxy.' Space Patrol was about to launch the SPX-1 spaceship to arrest the pirates when we realized that the ship had gone missing. Recorded camera footage showed that the last people seen entering the SPX-1 were two young children. We found their mothers and learned that the names of the boys are Thomas and Tryphone."

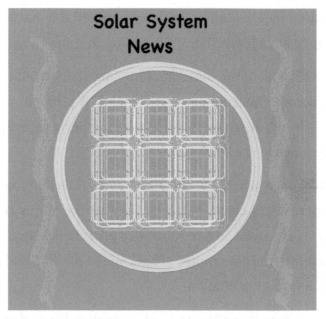

The reporter continued, "This young fellow may be in real big trouble from the pirates so Space Patrol officers have been sent in search of both the pirates and the children."

"The pirate might look like a normal pirate captain inside his ship. But he is considered the biggest, baddest pirate who has ever existed. He can dent a metal spaceship with one punch with his fist without hurting himself. "

"Tryphone! That pirate sounds like the pirate we just saw!" I said.

"You're right! He sure does," said Tryphone.

"We shall defeat them and become famous!" I said. "I think we can destroy their ship with our ship's lasers. If that doesn't work, then we will arm ourselves with all of the weapons we can find on this ship. We will then board their ship, and destroy their control panel where they can control their ship. We must keep plenty of distance between us and them and have our weapons aimed at them the entire time."

"Then we can quickly call the Space Patrol Military!" said Tryphone.

CHAPTER 7

Follow the Clues

"There should be some way to find them," I told Tryphone. This was a mystery. I am the detective and will use my detective skills.

"Okay, we know that they are pirates so where would they go? Aha! Pirates always want money, free money. Which planet has the most valuable metals?" I asked. "Tryphone, gimme the laptop. Wait no, a professional detective would use a full-size computer. You know what, I'll use the ship's computer."

Tryphone turned the closest monitor to face me.

"There. Professional." I searched "Which space thingy has the most gold?" and the ship's computer answered that the Psyche asteroid that was between Mars and Jupiter contained the most metal and all of that metal was worth $700,000,000,000,000,000,000, aka seven hundred quin-illion dollars.

When Tryphone saw the answer on the monitor, he said, "I just remembered, Neptune and Uranus rain diamonds!"

"Let's go to the Psyche asteroid first," I said.

"Okay," he replied.

We located Psyche and set the spaceship on autopilot toward the asteroid. On the way, so many asteroids, comets, and small rocks about the size of a human's head were hurtling toward us that at one point, moving, dodging, or just staying on course without getting hit was impossible!

Now, using my detective skills, I could tell that this was no usual, and something was wrong. I had to inspect these rocks. So I turned on the testing drill. Here is how it looked:

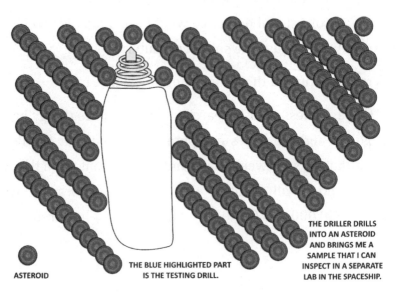

ASTEROID

THE BLUE HIGHLIGHTED PART IS THE TESTING DRILL.

THE DRILLER DRILLS INTO AN ASTEROID AND BRINGS ME A SAMPLE THAT I CAN INSPECT IN A SEPARATE LAB IN THE SPACESHIP.

When I inspected a few rock samples, using a scientific inspecting device, I figured out that these rocks contained lots of metal minerals. I'm calling them rocks because they were the same size as normal-sized rocks on Earth or Mars. The size and amount of these "rocks" all together could only be the result of some sort of extremely intense drilling.

"The pirates are drilling the Psyche asteroid!" I screamed.

"Full speed ahead!" Tryphone yelled.

As we dashed through the "rocks," we constantly scanned for the pirates. Once we reached the Psyche asteroid, we were surprised to find nothing but small "rocks" left, and something flat and brownish-white. Wearing my spacesuit and a rope tied around my waist, I went out to see what it was. With Tryphone holding the other end of the rope, I grabbed the flat object that seemed to be made of paper or parchment.

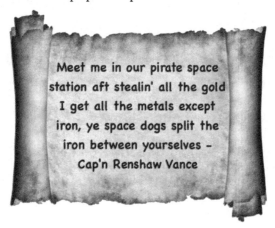

Meet me in our pirate space station aft stealin' all the gold I get all the metals except iron, ye space dogs split the iron between yourselves -
Cap'n Renshaw Vance

Once I was back inside the ship, we inspected the paper. A map was also included.

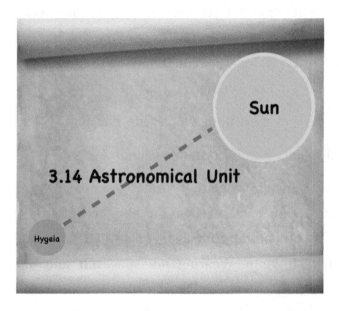

"We should go to Hygeia—the smallest dwarf planet—where their space station is before they get to Neptune or Uranus," I said.

"Thomas, I just figured out that it rains diamonds on Jupiter and Saturn, too! And the sun contains two and a half trillion tons of them!" said Tryphone.

"Well, first we go to Jupiter," I said.

"But *how* are we going to go there?" asked Tryphone. "Our ship will get destroyed when the diamonds start raining!"

"No worries, we're safe," I answered. "Our spaceship and our suits are apparently made out of wurtzite boron nitride, which is a metal that is stronger than diamond! Onward to Jupiter!"

"Yes sir," said Tryphone.

Our ship took us there at full speed. Once we'd landed on Jupiter, we realized that we couldn't possibly search the whole planet on foot or we would get lost (plus, it would take a really long time). Also, the diamonds were hitting our heads pretty hard. So, we got back into our ship and did a scan to see if any humans were already on Jupiter. The scan result said no.

Then, we headed to Saturn to check. The scan was still negative, so we turned on the ship's special heat shield, and sped off toward the Sun. Nobody detected there, either. We were very exhausted, but continued on to check Neptune. Our answer was still no.

We were about to give up, but after checking the planet Uranus, two humans were finally detected. "Yes! Let's go!" I screamed. "It must be Captain Vance, and the master gunner."

We landed the spaceship behind them and a little far away.

CHAPTER 8

The Battle of the Diamond World

"**Q**uick! Suit up!" I yelled. "Get your lonsdaleite sword! Get your lonsdaleite minigun! Get your lonsdaleite lasers! Get your lonsdaleite laser gun!"

If you're wondering what in the world lonsdaleite is, it's a celestial diamond even stronger than wurtzite boron nitride (w-BN). We will be using it in our two-vs-two battle against the pirates. We can break their w-BN space suit armor with our lonsdaleite weapons. In case you're also wondering how we will battle them on a different planet, the simple answer is that our space suits are very high tech and protect us from harmful gravity, atmosphere, and all of that stuff.

The two pirates were collecting the diamonds and didn't seem to even notice us. "Quick," I told Tryphone, "shoot all of your guns and lasers at their weapons while I aim all of my guns and lasers at their suits."

Before we were able to shoot at them, they quickly flew up into the air using their space boots. Then they turned around and shot at us with their guns. We just stood there as the diamond ammo bounced off of our suits.

"Wha'? How's this possible? This ain't fair. Belay that, aren' ye two the wee weak sprogs from a few years ago? Defeat 'em! the captain yelled to his master gunner.

As they both kept shooting at us, we started getting hurt. We put up our nuclear pasta shield (the strongest thing in the whole universe; even a supernova can't destroy it), and their weapons could no longer harm or touch us. The diamond ammo turned into dust after hitting the shield.

Then we were shocked to see supernovas hurtling toward us. They had opened portals facing us so that supernovas would come through and blast us. We had to keep changing the position of our super heavy shield, because when it blocked a supernova, we were pushed backward, and we had a hard time holding on to the shield.

We thought we might have a chance by throwing our nuclear pasta shield at them, but it was so heavy! And even if we were able to throw it, it wouldn't even make it halfway because there's no way we could throw it very fast. If we somehow magically managed a miracle by throwing the shield

far enough, they might dodge it. Then we wouldn't have a shield and would be at their mercy! But if it did reach them, we also didn't want to end their lives. We just wanted to capture them to arrest them.

We had to retreat; that was our only chance! We ran back to the spaceship and blasted off. From the sky, we started firing everything: missiles, cannons, and fire bombs. Because we didn't want to kill the pirates, we decided to use fire bombs instead of a nuke. We also threw smoke bombs so they couldn't see us. But we could see them when we wore our cool infrared vision glasses.

We then realized that defeating them from above wouldn't work because if some of the pirate's diamond ammo hit one of our missiles while it was still close to our ship, the explosion could impact us, or one of our missiles would be wasted.

After talking about it, we decided that we should land, then take them on separately. I would face the captain and Tryphone would face the master gunner. Tryphone would hold his lonsdaleite great sword in his right hand and his lonsdaleite long sword in his left hand. I would use my lonsdaleite polearm with my right hand and my lonsdaleite whip with my left hand. We would do two one-on-one battles in different areas to keep the pirates separated.

"Tryphone! Get ready, we're landing," I said. As we were landing, we fixed our infrared glasses over our suit helmets very tightly. Once we were on the ground, we tried to separate the two pirates.

"Hey! Mr. Renshy Pants! Over here!" I screamed at Captain Renshaw Vance.

"Hey! Noob Gunner! You literally lost to a little kid!" Tryphone screamed at the master gunner. The two pirates got mad and each went after one of us in opposite directions. Our plan to separate them worked.

CHAPTER 9

Thomas vs. Captain Renshaw Vance

Look, fighting pirates with a partner is one thing, but fighting the solar system's biggest, baddest pirate captain by yourself is a *whole 'nother story.*

"Shiver me timbers, ye scurvy, rum-running coxswain! Ye can nah beat me up, ye wee sprog. Come on! Attack me if ye can! Ye aren't stronger than me! I be also way smarter than ye! Once I defeat ye, I will get lots o' doubloons 'n equipment. I needs yer booty!" yelled the captain.

As I charged, I tried to show him who the boss was, but he dodged it and slammed his w-BN sword right on my neck. Luckily, I turned and avoided the full power of the blow, but it still probably fractured my spine. As spasms surged through my body, I felt a sharp, stabbing pain sting my nerves. Tears poured from my eyes and I couldn't bear the pain. The pain just triggered me! I was so angry, full of hatred, and full of pain as I focused all of my power into my hand. I felt like I was zapped except, the zap charged me up! Using all the power I had left, charged at the pirate's head with confidence and strength and knocked him down with my polearm!

"Blast ye! That hurts! This ain't fair! I will destroy ye! I will blow ye down! I will crush ye t' pieces! No, this can nah be! Ye shall pay!" yelled the captain as he fell to the ground.

But the next second, he stood up! I was really surprised. Then it started to rain diamonds again. This was my chance! I batted all the diamonds at the pirate until he was forced to move back disturbed and annoyed.

Then, I used my whip to whip his face a few times and the fourth time, I wrapped the whip around him very tightly. Then started tugging on the whip so that it would squeeze him. I pulled the whip toward me and he fell to the ground at my feet. I made sure that he wouldn't be able to move, then I put my foot on his head and with lots of confidence, I said loud and clear, "Today, have defeated the fiercest pirate of all!" And with that, I put my foot back down on the ground.

Finally, I took my polearm and started bonking him on the head, whacking him all around his body, and just beating him up At the same time, I was screaming "Hiiiiya! Booya! Oh yeah? Take that! In your face! Punch punch punch!" And I also screamed a million other things that made the pirate feel like he'd lost to a baby who didn't even have common sense.

But, apparently, that seemed to trigger his anger again. With all his might, he screamed and wiggled enough to loosen the whip around him so he could get up. He stood up and started to punch and kick me! He sure knew how to fight like a martial artist.

I dropped my weapons and started boxing with him. I punched him in the face and kicked him in the stomach. That seemed to be a very powerful and effective combo. He then took me down and started beating me up. I quickly got up from between his legs, and carried him on my back almost like I was giving him a piggyback ride!

But why would I even do such a thing? That would just harm me! He could just punch the back of my head and boom! My neck would be broken, I wouldn't be able to see anymore, my vision would be gone!

As he made an attempt to punch me, I quickly threw him to the ground at an angle that would make his fist punch the ground instead of me. Some very sharp and hard diamonds were lying on the ground. As he punched the ground, he broke his arm and screamed, "Oh! That hurts! It aches so much! I reckon I broke me hand! Argh! Help! I can nah bear it! I will crush ye, ye fork-faced kilick brained, bilge rat!"

To my surprise, he was still able to get up. He quickly took out his cutlass and started slashing it at me. I retreated toward where I'd dropped my weapons, and re-armed myself with my polearm and whip. I kept whipping my whip at him, so he kept his distance.

That actually ended up backfiring because he apparently also had a pistol. He started shooting at me and since I had no shield, I kept dodging, but eventually took a hit which hurt even with my armor-suit on. He finally ran out of ammo for his pistol.

Unfortunately, he also had grenades! They kept hitting me even when I tried to duck and evade them. I was so exhausted, my muscles were sore, and I was tired.

But as they say—well actually, that's what I say from now on—just when you are about to give up, you get a bright idea. (I'll make it my saying when I return from my mission and become famous.) My bright idea was that *his* suit had a glass helmet, but my suit helmet is made of higher tech.

Simple: I'll either throw my polearm directly at his helmet or whip my whip at it to crack it, and then the oxygen will leak out of his helmet and he'll faint. I didn't have much time! After this, I needed to check on Tryphone, and the captain was about to get ultra violent any second now.

Without thinking, I ran towards the pirate and whipped my whip at his glass helmet. I heard it crack. He started suffocating and once his eyes closed as he fainted, to keep him alive, I put an oxygen mask over his nose. I tied him up and disarmed him. After making sure he wasn't in danger, I got him onto an anti-gravity cart because he was too heavy to carry. Then I took him to the spaceship to lock him in a huge cage.

CHAPTER 10

Tryphone vs. the Master Gunner

Hello, my name is Tryphone. Thomas has been narrating this story so far, but right now, he is still battling the pirate captain. I wonder how he's doing?

Suddenly the master gunner said, "Come on! Jus' belay that 'fore we start fightin', ye will lose, ye're jus' a wee sprog. Me boss vants yer head. He has a collection, but if ye jus' belay that now, 'll keep ye safe. Look, I be a kinder space dog than me boss. I don't vants t' hurt ye."

Now, he was getting a little too suspicious. I unsheathed both of my swords and charged toward him. Because he was actually pretty mart or because he was the master *gunner*, he started firing his minigun at me to keep me from charging forward. I had to dodge the bullets and started to move backward.

But I had to stand my ground. I crossed my two swords to reate a thick shield and advanced slowly, step by step. The

diamonds on the ground made it difficult to walk. Thoma
wouldn't have struggled with this because his boots were
designed to create little air-shields between the bottom of the
boots and the diamonds so he could walk smoothly.

I kept tripping on the diamonds, which unfortunately, caused
me to fall down heavily on the pointy diamonds. Luckily, my
helmet and suit saved me from injury. He walked over to where I'd
fallen and started firing his minigun at my chest, from directly
above me.

This affected both of us. Each bullet he shot at me (at least a
hundred in those three seconds) hit me but also bounced off of my
suit and then hit his suit then bounced off of his suit and so on. In
less than a few seconds, all the bullets hit each other and ***BOOM***
There was an explosion. Both of us were blown back and I think
my toe was probably broken.

Fortunately for me, it looked like the master gunner broke hi
right arm. The broken toe didn't hurt at all. *Ouch!* Okay, when the
bottom of my toe touches my shoe, it hurt a lot. So, lifting my
broken toe, I ran at the master gunner again. He was unable to
shoot with a broken right arm! As I charged, I felt pride surging
through my body.

I stabbed my great sword at him and it punctured his suit
Then, I stabbed my long sword at his helmet and watched hi
helmet break. He screamed, "Mama! Help!" then closed his eye

nd seemed to faint. I put an oxygen mask over his nose and tied him up.

I put the master gunner on an anti-gravity cart so I could take him to the spaceship and lock him in a large cage.

CHAPTER 11

Friends Reunite

Right after I locked the captain's cage and everything seemed to be safe, I thought that I should collect some stupendous diamonds for my family. But when I was about to exit the spaceship to collect the diamonds, I saw a figure coming toward me, pulling something. The person looked male—it could either be the master gunner or Tryphone. Just in case, I took out my polearm and whip.

The person waved his hand, and I saw that it was actually Tryphone! He had captured the master gunner and put him on an anti-gravity cart too. We were tremendously relieved and overjoyed to see each other again. He locked the master gunner up in the cage next to the captain's cage. We stood in front of the two cages and stared at the two pirates. They looked like they were about to recover consciousness, so we decided to add a teensy bit of spice to the victory.

Once they were conscious again, I told Tryphone, "And then I punched the pirate like this! Hiiiiya!" and then hit myself in the head and said, "Ow! That hurts!" just like a little baby so that the pirates would feel very degraded that they'd lost to such morons.

Then, we started playing like babies in front of them. The captain said, "We lost t' wee sprogs! They don't even know how t' punch! They play like wee sprogs! We, the best pirate band, lost t' sprogs! May Corsair bring us mercy. I shall offer me leg fer mercy. Corsair! May Ramsey be wit' us!"

We both laughed. The captain's face got very red and he tried to break out of his cage but couldn't. We both sat down right in front of the cages and chatted, had snacks, and had some fun. We played video games and real-world games like tag and rock-paper-scissors. We also played coconut, fireball, cowboy, hide and seek, chess, and many other fun games.

We enjoyed making fun of the pirates, shared stories, talked about what might be happening back home on Mars or what we might do once we returned. We showed off our weapons and our fighting skills. We even did a friendly, mini battle with our armor and weapons.

We had lots and lots of fun. We freaked out the pirates and made them jealous. We also told each other how our different battles with the pirates went and what happened. When we were playing tag, Tryphone suddenly fell and started crying. I asked him what happened and he said that he'd broken his toe during his battle.

We used the ship's Auto Bone-Regenerator to heal his toe and my spine. The A.B.R. injected us with a serum that regenerates the broken part of a bone. We were soon back to normal in no time.

Finally, we decided that it was time to go back home. We double checked the pirates' cages to make sure they had no way of escaping or causing any trouble.

I sat in the pilot's chair and set the course toward Mars up on the screen. I was just waiting for Tryphone when I heard the pirates screaming from where they were locked up. I could hear Tryphone yelling back at them, so I rushed to see what was going on.

Tryphone was trying to quiet them down so the noise wouldn't distract us. With my help, we were able to cover their mouths and also tied their arms and legs behind them for good measure. **NOW** we were ready to blast off and head back home!

CHAPTER 12

On Our Way Back Home

Woohoo! We were on our way back home! As we blasted off, we experienced a little disturbance from the diamond rain. So, Tryphone temporarily opened a compartment in the front of the spaceship to collect lots and lots of diamonds for both of our families.

After we left Uranus's atmosphere, we were surrounded by a lot of dark asteroids. They looked like ice boulders and ice chunks that had rock particles, dust, and parts of other asteroids attached to them.

After a great deal of focus, energy, and time, we finally passed through the asteroid field. Wait, nope, we ran into another layer of them. They were actually Uranus's rings! Uranus has thirteen small rings. We struggled to keep going, and finally passed through ten of the rings. Each ring was harder and harder to escape from, partially because I was getting more tired and sleepy by the minute, but also because each ring was full of bigger, stronger, and more dangerous ice boulders and ice chunks than the last one.

We used our lasers to make way for our spaceship. Finally, we reached the thirteenth ring but needed to recharge the laser.

It took an entire day for the lasers to recharge and while they were recharging, I slept for six hours with Tryphone keeping watch. Then Tryphone slept for six hours with me keeping watch. Finally, the lasers were fully recharged and we made our way through the thirteenth ring.

Of course, another obstacle found *us!* I immediately sped up after finally escaping the last ring but had forgotten about the twenty-seven small moons. I was about to crash into Uranus's largest moon, Titania! Tryphone and I quickly put the engines in reverse—me in the captain's chair and him in the co-pilot's seat. The ship was only about a mile away from Titania's surface when it fortunately halted.

We steered around the moon, cautiously. We continued on and reached Saturn. In orbit around the planet, we discovered another ship. When we got closer to it, we saw that it was a space pirate's ship.

We called them with our ship's transmitter and told them to surrender. We told them that the solar system's biggest, baddest pirate, Captain Vance, was our prisoner. They responded immediately, welcoming us aboard, and allowed us to capture them. When we continued on to each one of Saturn's 145 other moons, we found a pirate ship orbiting or already landed on every single one!

So we told the pirates on each one of those ships the same thing, and apparently they were so impressed and afraid of us, that they all surrendered too.

Well, now our ship was getting too crowded, so we put all the prisoners in the three big prisoner cages. This way we still had plenty of room in our ship, and the pirates couldn't hardly move and were suffering for all of the crimes they'd committed and trouble they had caused.

Next, we had to go to Hygeia because Captain Renshaw Vance's space station was somewhere near there. On our way, we had a very hard time dodging comets that were flying by. Our spaceship's fin was hit! Luckily, our spaceship had automatic mini-robots and machines to fix some kinds of damage. We just had to push the "Self-repair" button.

While the ship was repairing itself, and we were just sitting there in space, a lot of asteroids appeared. Even when pushed on by our spaceship's shield, they didn't move out of the way. And for some reason, the laser wasn't destroying them as they usually did, so we were surrounded by asteroids with no way out!

Our only option to escape seemed to be to call Solar System Patrol. But if we did that, no one would see us as such big heroes anymore. There had to be another solution! I turned the lasers to their highest level, and Tryphone operated the driller. Together we used the tools to drill the asteroids, one by one. To make a path to Hygeia, it took us approximately seven Martian days.

Once we reached Hygeia, we realized that we could've just gone around that clump of asteroids! We also discovered that Vance's space station was very close to Hygeia. It was also apparently just a huge spaceship. This could be useful.

We landed our spaceship inside the pirate's huge space station, in the spaceship parking garage. The station appeared to be deserted, so we found the control panel and set the space station's autopilot on course for Mars. Then we slept the whole way.

Finally, after a few days, we made it home!

CHAPTER 13

Home Sweet Home!

Once we reached Mars, we decided to land the space station on the huge field next to the Space Patrol Base. As we were landing, hundreds of soldiers aimed their weapons and defense lasers at us. Probably because of the pirate symbol on the space station.

Once we landed, through the radio and the speakers on the outside of the space station, I said, "Hello, Space Patrol, this is Thomas. Yeah, the kid who blasted off with this spaceship several days ago. Oh, sorry, we traveled at lightspeed, so for you guys here on Mars, it's been several years. Anyway... I'VE GOT GREAT NEWS! Tryphone and I captured all the space pirates! I will now open the door. Do not fire!"

Then, I opened the door and walked down the ramp with all my armor on and my shield, just in case they fired. Tryphone came out behind me. We waited for a few seconds with our hands up, then slowly and cautiously, we removed our helmets to show our faces.

The soldiers all lowered their weapons because they could see we weren't a threat. I screamed, "Yahoo! Yay! Yeah! Let's go! Home sweet home!" Tryphone shouted too, and punched his fist in the air.

I told the soldier in charge to follow us back to where the pirates were locked up. Then, with all of the soldiers watching and cheering, we drug all of the pirates, along with Captain Vance, out of the cages and out of the spaceship. I finally got to turn in the pirates! Tryphone and I were heroes! The pirates were all handcuffed and put in Space Patrol trucks and driven off to jail. The last thing we heard Captain Vance say before he was shoved into a van was, "Ye will pay fer dis! Ye haven't won yet! I'll surely get ye next time! I'll be back! Ye got only a wee win. 'twill be my turn soon. Enjoy yer victory!"

Everyone was very happy and excited. Both my parents and Tryphone's parents soon arrived! Space Patrol held a ceremony for us, with cameras and reporters. As a reward, we were granted $3,789,987.

We gave our parents great big hugs when we saw them. Everyone shed some tears, then our parents started to scold us for being naughty, while also praising us for our heroic acts.

Sometimes, I just don't understand my parents. They say one thing, but then the opposite. That is just the mystery of parents.

My mom said, "Aww sweetie, are you okay? Are you okay, my poor little darling? What happened to you out there?" and for the first time—and maybe the last time—in my whole life, I was glad to hear that and hugged my mom even tighter.

The school bullies (several years older, now), surprisingly, also showed up at the ceremony. Benignus came up to me and said, "Good job, you aren't a weakling after all!" That made me feel proud of myself.

I gave a speech and told a story about everything that had happened, including every single small detail of our journey.

"Ladies and gentlemen, I, Thomas, the protector of the solar system, am here with you all. This is a once-in-a-blue-moon chance for you all to meet me and my co-pilot. I have to say that saving the world is not an easy task, but as they say, hard work pays off, so always listen to your conscience and do what's right. Thank you!"

The day we returned was awesome. Finally, with a huge smile on my face, I went to bed.

That night, I had a dream. Some strange man was standing in a high-tech laboratory in outer space.

In my dream, he said to me, "You have defeated one of my minions, but not me. You will fall at my feet. But only if you accept my challenge."

I freaked out then suddenly woke up to see that I was still in my room. The room was pitch black and I couldn't see anything. I sat up, sweat dripping down my face. That was a very intense nightmare. Maybe I should call Tryphone? No, I think I should just go back to sleep.

But for some reason I was still scared. Who was that man? Gasping for air, my head felt dizzy, I felt terrible, and slowly, my mind was shattered into oblivion.

About the Author

Amrrut Saravanakumaran is passionate about reading and writing, with a particular interest in mathematics, science and history. He is also skilled in coding with JavaScript and Python. Residing in Milpitas, California, Amrrut enjoys the Percy Jackson and the Olympians series by Rick Riordan. Outside of academics, he participates in karate and table tennis classes and has a strong affinity for writing essays. Amrrut believes in the value of hard work and enjoys expressing his creativity through drawing, painting, and coloring. His favorite animals include cats, German shepherds, and duck-billed platypuses.

Made in the USA
Las Vegas, NV
24 September 2024